GEORGE AND THE DRAGON

CHRIS WORMELL

RED FOX

Far, far away in the high, high mountains

in a deep, deep valley in a dark, dark cave...

there lived a mighty dragon.

He could fly higher than the clouds

and faster than all the birds.

He could burn down a forest

with a blast of his fiery breath.

He could smash a castle wall

with a flick of his mighty tail.

And he could brush away an army

with a sweep of his monstrous wing.

There was nothing so fierce and so terrible
as the mighty dragon.

But he had a secret. A big secret, well, actually, a very small secret...

he was terrified of mice!

Which was a pity, because that very day a
mouse moved into the cave just next door.

His name was George.

Now, George didn't much care for the cave next door. It was cold and dark and draughty.

The previous owner had been a bat,
so the fixtures and furnishings were
most inconvenient.

And the nearest cheese shop was
miles and miles away.

George was feeling rather miserable.
And to make matters worse...

he had NO SUGAR for his tea!

'I know,' said George, 'I'll just pop next
door and see if I can borrow some.'
So he did.

'I say, you couldn't loan me a couple of lumps of sugar, could you?' asked George.

'AAAAAAAAAGH!' screamed the dragon.

And fled.

'Oh, blow,' groaned George. 'No tea, then.'

But George did get his tea after all, with
two lumps of sugar. And he got cheese, too.
And nuts and berries and biscuits and

crackers and cream cheese sandwiches and
jelly and ice cream and fairy cakes with
pink icing and...

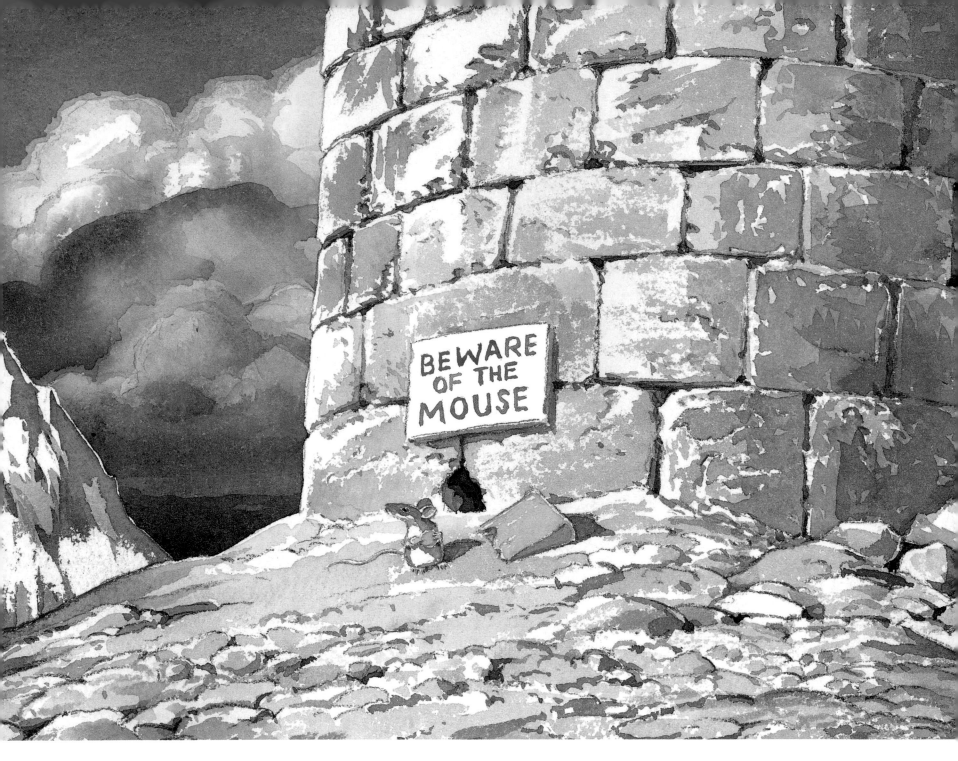

a cosy little hole in the castle wall.

To John and Terry

GEORGE AND THE DRAGON
A RED FOX BOOK 978 1 862 30213 6 (from January 2007)
1 862 30213 8

First published in Great Britain by Jonathan Cape,
an imprint of Random House Children's Books

Jonathan Cape edition published 2002
Red Fox edition published 2003
This edition published 2006

3 5 7 9 10 8 6 4 2

Red Fox Books are published by Random House Children's Books,
61-63 Uxbridge Road, London W5 5SA,
a division of The Random House Group Ltd,
in Australia by Random House Australia (Pty) Ltd,
20 Alfred Street, Milsons Point, Sydney, NSW 2061, Australia,
in New Zealand by Random House New Zealand Ltd,
18 Poland Road, Glenfield, Auckland 10, New Zealand,
and in South Africa by Random House (Pty) Ltd,
Isle of Houghton, Corner Boundary Road & Carse O'Gowrie,
Houghton 2198, South Africa

THE RANDOM HOUSE GROUP Limited Reg. No. 954009
www.kidsatrandomhouse.co.uk

A CIP catalogue record for this book is available from the British Library.

Printed in China